Page 2

Page 3

Page 4

Page 5

Page 6

Page 7

D1486571

© Disney

Page 7

Page 6

Page 8

Page 9

Page 11

Page 10

Page 13

Page 12

Page 15

Page 16

Page 19

Page 20

Page 22

Sparkling

Sticker Dress-Up

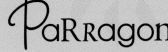

Bath · New York · Cologne · Melbourne · Delhi
Hong Kong · Shenzhen · Singapore

Young Princess Anna

When Anna was young, she spent lots of time playing in her bedroom. Dress her in a pretty dress and shoes. Add her favorite doll, too!

Place your stickers in the following order: dress, shoes, doll.

Young Princess Elsa

When Elsa was young, she tried to keep her powers hidden. Dress Princess Elsa and add her favorite doll.

Place your stickers in the following order: dress, shoes, doll.

3

Sisters Forever

Before Elsa accidentally hurt Anna with her magic, the sisters loved to play together in the snow. Dress young Elsa in her warm winter play clothes.

Place your stickers in the following order: socks, shoes, dress.

Anna used to love playing outside in the summertime, too. Dress young Anna in her pretty summer play clothes.

Place your stickers in the following order: dress, shoes.

5

Coronation Day

It's the day of Elsa's coronation, and Princess Anna can't wait to welcome everyone to Arendelle! Use your stickers to make Anna look beautiful.

Place your stickers in the following order: dress, necklace.

Elsa is worried about accidentally revealing her powers at the ceremony. Help her practice holding the royal orb and scepter in her hands without freezing them. Help her to get dressed, too.

Place your stickers in the following order: shoes, dress, crown, orb, scepter.

To the North Mountain!

Princess Anna must trek to the North Mountain to find Queen Elsa and save Arendelle from eternal winter. Dress Anna in warm, cozy clothes.

Place your stickers in the following order: boots, dress and cape, gloves, hat.

Anna has found someone
to help her on her way.
Kristoff is a kind mountain man.
Use your stickers to dress him.

Place your stickers in the following order: clothes, boots, gloves.

Frozen Friends

Anna and Kristoff have met a funny snowman called Olaf! Use your stickers to put him together on this page.

Place your stickers in the following order: body, feet, head, arms, buttons, hair, carrot nose.

Kristoff's best friend is a reindeer called Sven. Give him some antlers and a basket of treats—he loves carrots!

Place your stickers in the following order: antlers, box of carrots.

Old Friends

Kristoff and Sven have been friends since they were young. Dress little Kristoff and add baby Sven to the scene.

Place your stickers in the following order: clothes, boots, Sven.

"I Love Heat!"

It may seem strange, but Olaf longs to experience summer! Complete his dream by giving him a sun hat and other things he might need for a day at the beach.

Place your stickers in the following order: hat, drink, bucket and shovel, beach ball.

The Ice Palace

Queen Elsa has created a magnificent
ice palace on the North Mountain.
Find her enchanting icy gown, shoes, and
a sparkle of magic on your sticker sheet,
and add them to the picture.

If you could create
your own ice palace,
how many rooms
would it have?

What color
would your
dream
dress be?

If you could have
any magical power,
what would
you choose?

Place your stickers in the following order: shoes, dress, magical sparkles.

A Summer Party

Arendelle has been saved from eternal winter. Anna is getting ready for a summer party. Help her to get dressed and add long braids to her hair.

Place your stickers in the following order: shoes, dress, hair.

16

Kristoff is invited to the party, too. Dress him in his best clothes so he can dance with Princess Anna.

Place your stickers in the following order: clothes, boots.

17

A Masked Ball

Princess Anna is getting ready for a masked ball. Find her dress and accessories on your sticker sheet and add her lovely costume.

What color dress would you choose?

What kind of mask would you wear to a masked ball?

What color is Anna's mask?

Place your stickers in the following order: shoes, dress, mask, necklace, fan.

What's Different?

Olaf is dreaming of summer! Can you spot six differences in the second picture below? Add a bucket-and-shovel sticker for each difference you find.

Answers:

Follow Your Heart

Anna, Kristoff, and Olaf are searching for Queen Elsa. Spot two pictures that are exactly the same, then use your sparkly stickers to decorate the page!

c

b

e

d

Family Forever

Use your stickers to complete this picture of Queen Elsa, Princess Anna, and their best friends.

Answer:

Icy Patterns

Do you know what comes next in each of these pretty patterns? Place the correct sparkly sticker at the end of each row.

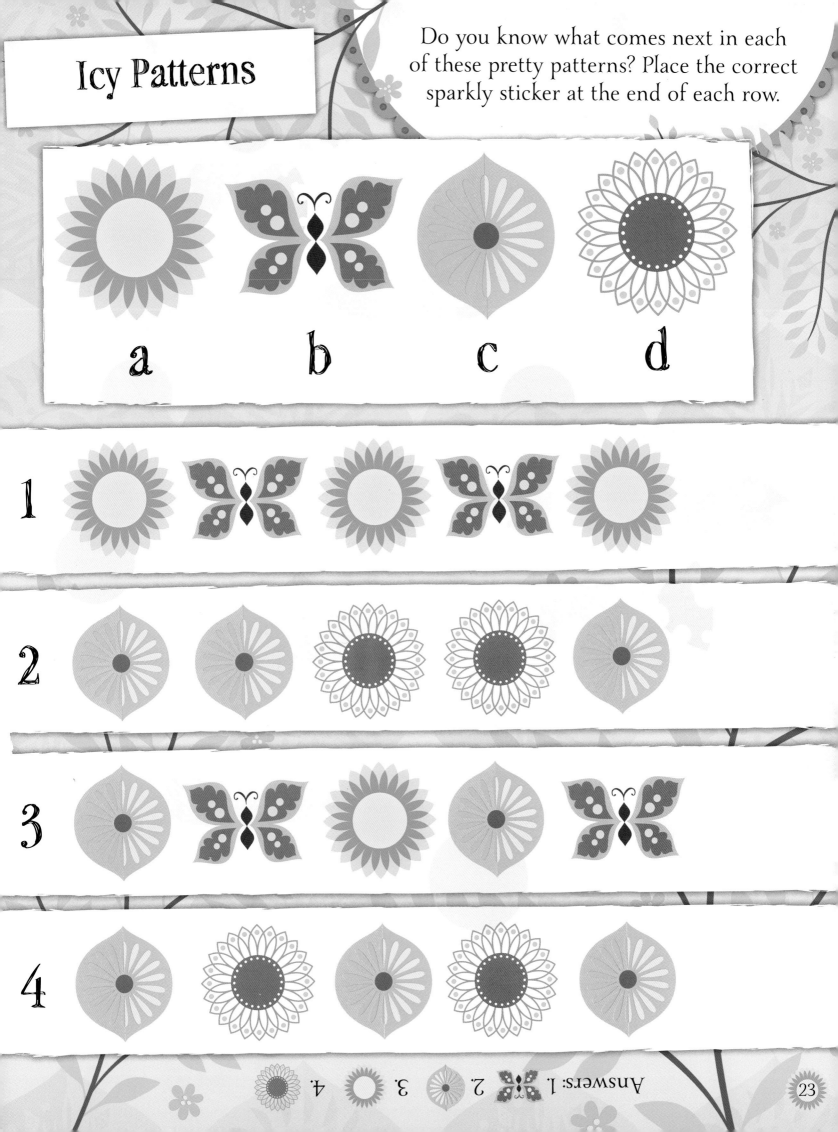

a   b   c   d

1

2

3

4

Answers: 1. 2. 3. 4.

Queen Elsa's New Gown

Draw and color a sparkling new dress for Queen Elsa. Make it icy, elegant, and beautiful!